MY DOG
and the
GREEN SOCK
MYSTERY

by David A. Adler
illustrated by Dick Gackenbach

Holiday House/New York

Text copyright © 1986 by David A. Adler
Illustrations copyright © 1986 by Dick Gackenbach
All rights reserved
Printed in the United States of America
First Edition

Library of Congress Cataloging-in-Publication Data

Adler, David A.
    My dog and the green sock mystery.

    Summary: Jennie's dog solves the mystery of the
disappearing objects at her friend Andy's house.
    [1. Dogs—Fiction. 2. Lost and found possessions—
Fiction. 3. Mystery and detective stories]
I. Gackenbach, Dick, ill. II. Title.
PZ7.A2615MW   1986   [E]   85-14145
ISBN 0-8234-0590-7

To my cousins, LISA and SETH BROWN

My name is Jennie.
This is my dog.
My dog has white hair
with black spots,
a long tail and is really smart.
She solves mysteries.
I couldn't think of a good name
for my dog,
so I just call her My Dog.

One afternoon I was outside
playing with My Dog.
I threw a ball across the yard.
My Dog barked.
"Get it," I said.
"Get the ball."

My Dog ran to the ball.
But she ran past it.
She ran out of my yard.
When she didn't come back
I went looking for her.

My Dog is smart
but she gets lost a lot.
I found My Dog
running around my neighbor's house.
She was looking for me.
I brought My Dog back to my yard.
I was about to throw the ball again
when I saw Andy.
"I need you to help me
solve a mystery," Andy said.
"Things have disappeared from my room.
First it was my green sock.
Then some baseball cards disappeared.
And now my homework is gone."
My Dog barked.
I knew what she wanted me to ask Andy.
So I did.

"Where was your sock
  before it disappeared?" I asked.
"It was on my bed
  with all my other socks," Andy said.
"I was just about to put them away."
  My Dog barked again.

She wanted to ask Andy
where his baseball cards
and homework were.
But My Dog can't talk.
So I asked Andy,
"Where were your baseball cards
and homework?"
"My baseball cards were on my bed.
My homework was on the floor
on top of my book bag.
I had just finished doing it.
I went to the kitchen
and had some milk and cookies.
When I came back to my room
the homework and baseball cards were gone.
I need that homework," Andy said.

My Dog wagged her tail and barked.
I laughed.
I knew what she wanted to say,
so I said it for her.
"My Dog has already solved your mystery.
Lots of kids are sloppy.
Just clean up your room
and you'll find your things."

"Well, I'm not a sloppy kid," Andy said.
"My room doesn't need to be cleaned up."
I looked at Andy.
His shoelaces were tied.
His shirt and pants
didn't have wrinkles.
He was right.
He was not a sloppy kid.

My Dog barked again.
I told Andy, "My Dog says
you must take us to your house.
She will solve your mystery."
"Ha," Andy said.
"Your dog doesn't solve mysteries.
You do.
Your dog is dumb."
"She is not," I told him.
"She's real dumb," Andy said.
"I saw her chew a stick once.
She thought it was a bone.
And your dog is always getting lost."
I told Andy,
"Just take us to your house.
My Dog will prove she's smart.
My Dog will solve your mystery."

As we walked,
My Dog stopped at a trash can.
The lid was off.
My Dog put her head in
and sniffed the trash.
I told Andy,
"She's looking for clues."
"She's looking for a bone
  or a stick to eat," Andy said.

Before I walked into Andy's house,
I wiped my feet.
My Dog wiped her feet too,
all four of them.
As soon as we were inside,
My Dog barked.
"Tell her to be quiet," Andy said.
"My baby brother might be sleeping."

Andy's mother came out of the kitchen.
A little boy was crawling behind her.
"You don't have to be quiet,"
Andy's mother said.
"Billy isn't sleeping."
She went into the kitchen again.
Billy followed her.
"Now come to my room," Andy said,
"and I'll show you
where I lost my green sock,
my baseball cards and my homework."
Andy's room was really neat.
On the shelves, little toy people,
toy cars, and wooden blocks
were standing in straight rows.

I held onto My Dog.
I didn't want her
to mess up Andy's room.

"The homework was on the floor
  right on top of my book bag,"
  Andy said.
"And the sock and baseball cards
  were on my bed.
  I was just about to put them away."
  There was nothing on Andy's floor,
  no papers, no pencils and no clothing.
  Andy really *is* neat.
  I looked at his bed.
  It was covered with a blanket.
  My Dog barked.
  She wanted me to look
  under the blanket.
"I'm sorry," I told Andy
  as I pulled off the blanket,
"but I have to do this."
  Under the blanket was a sheet.
  I pulled off the sheet
  and found another sheet.

I pulled that one off too.
But I didn't find
the green sock, the baseball cards
or the missing homework.

"Look what you did to my bed,"
Andy said.
He began to put the sheets
back on the bed.
Billy crawled into Andy's room.
He was holding a piece of bread.
My Dog barked.
"Keep that dog away from my brother,"
Andy said as he picked up Billy.
My Dog barked again.

She pulled away from me
and jumped at the bread.
My Dog knocked over the desk chair.
The toy people, cars and blocks
fell off the shelves.

"Look what your dog did," Andy said.
He put Billy down.
Then Andy began to pick up the toys.
Billy crawled out of the room.
I grabbed My Dog's collar
before she could chase after Billy.
My Dog pulled me out into the hall.
Billy was there.
We followed him to a room with a crib
and lots of baby toys.
"This must be Billy's room,"
I told My Dog.

Billy crawled to his crib.
He put the bread under the crib.
Then he crawled to his toys
and began to play with them.
My Dog pulled away from me.
She put her head under Billy's crib
and pulled out the bread.
My Dog ate the bread.

Then she put her head under the crib
and pulled out another piece of bread
and a green sock.
I looked under Billy's crib.
I found a slipper, a torn book,
a mitten and a spoon.
I also found baseball cards
and Andy's homework.

"Hey Andy!" I called.
"My Dog has done it again.
My Dog has solved your mystery."
When Andy came into Billy's room,
I showed him Billy's hiding place
and all the things he had there.
And then I said,
"My Dog isn't dumb.

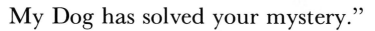
My Dog has solved your mystery."

Andy picked up his sock,
his baseball cards and his homework.
Then he looked at My Dog.
She was still eating the bread.

Andy said, "Maybe your dog is smart.
Or maybe your dog is dumb
and just likes to eat bread."

When we left Andy's house,
My Dog ran ahead.
When I got home My Dog wasn't there,
so I went looking for My Dog.
She was lost again.